Five reasons why you'll love Mirabelle...

Mirabelle is magical
and mischievous!

Mirabelle is half
witch, half fairy, and
totally naughty!

She loves making
potions with her travelling
potion kit!

Mirabelle loves sprinkling
a sparkle of mischief
wherever she goes!

She has a
little baby dragon
called Violet!

If you could fly anywhere on a broomstick, where would you go?

I would go to the beach to play a bit, and then go back home.
– Ariana

I'd go to different countries I've never been before.
– Bella

To candy floss world.
  – Frances

I would go to Candy Land where fairies, mermaids and unicorns live, a magic world where anything is possible.
  – Iris

To the jungle where sloths live.
  – Miriam

I would fly to Unicorn School.
  – Ellie

Family Tree

My Mum
Seraphina Starspell

My brother
Wilbur Starspell

My Dad
Alvin Starspell

Me!
Mirabelle Starspell

Violet

Illustrated by Mike Love, based on
original artwork by Harriet Muncaster

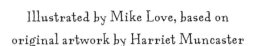

OXFORD
UNIVERSITY PRESS

Great Clarendon Street, Oxford OX2 6DP

Oxford University Press is a department of the University of Oxford.
It furthers the University's objective of excellence in research, scholarship, and
education by publishing worldwide. Oxford is a registered trade mark of Oxford
University Press in the UK and in certain other countries

First published 2021

British Library Cataloguing in Publication Data

Data available

ISBN: 978-0-19-277754-6

1 3 5 7 9 10 8 6 4 2

Printed in China

Paper used in the production of this book is a natural,
recyclable product made from wood grown in sustainable forests.
The manufacturing process conforms to the environmental
regulations of the country of origin.

From the world of  ISADORA MOON

MIRABELLE

Breaks the Rules

Harriet Muncaster

OXFORD
UNIVERSITY PRESS

Chapter ONE

It was the first day of a new term at witch school and I was up early, before anyone else in my family.

'Let's make breakfast for everyone,' I said to my pet dragon, Violet, as she fluttered in the air next to my ear. 'It will be a nice surprise!' Violet did a little snort and purple flames shot out of her snout. I

hurriedly batted them
away with a tea towel.
My mum gets funny about
scorch marks around the house.

I started to put bowls and plates
on the table, and put some bread in the
toaster for Mum. We all eat very different
breakfasts in my family. My mum is a
witch and eats all sorts of horrid things.
Her favourite breakfast is spider sprinkled
toast. My dad on the other hand, is a fairy.
He likes eating flower nectar yoghurt and
lots of green salads. Fairies love nature!

The toast popped and I reached for
Mum's jar of frizzled spiders.

'Yuck!' I said as I tipped a heap of

them onto her toast.

Next I put some yoghurt and flower petals into a bowl for Dad and then started to make mine and Wilbur's breakfast. Wilbur is half fairy just like me except he doesn't like to admit it.

He insists that he is a full wizard most of the time. I don't mind my fairy side so much, but I definitely feel more witch! That's why I decided to go to 'Miss Spindlewick's Witch School for Girls'.

As I was buttering Wilbur's toast my eye was drawn back to Mum's spider jar sitting on the counter. A naughty idea floated into my head.

'Go away!' I told it.

But the thought would not go away. My toes started tingling at the idea of mischief.

I pulled Mum's spider jar towards me

and used a fork to scoop out just one little crispy critter. I dropped it onto Wilbur's toast and then quickly slathered it over with jam. He would never know it was there until he felt it crunch in his mouth! I giggled at the thought of him discovering the spider. Both of us hate witch food.

'Breakfast time!' I called up the stairs.

★ ★ ★

'How thoughtful of you to make everyone breakfast Mirabelle,' said Dad as he tucked into his rose petal yoghurt. I smiled sweetly

and watched Wilbur from out of the corner of my eye.

'I hope this is a sign of things to come!' said Mum.

'What do you mean?' I asked.

'Well it's the first day of a new school term,' said Mum. 'I'm hoping you're starting as you mean to go on! I don't want to hear any more reports of mischief from your teacher this year.'

'Oh,' I said and felt my cheeks turn a tiny bit pink. Wilbur took another bite of his jammy toast.

Crunch.

I gulped. Mum

frowned. Wilbur stopped chewing for a moment and then his face turned very white. He spat his mouthful out onto his plate and stared, horrified at the spider legs sticking out of it.

'MIRABELLE!' he shouted angrily. Then he picked up the chewed up mouthful with the spider in it and threw it at me. I ducked just in time!

'Mirabelle!' said Mum and her eyes went very dark and glinty like they do when she's getting angry. But the corner of her mouth twitched slightly. My mum has a mischievous streak inside her too, though she does her best to hide it.

'Sorry,' I whispered, but it was hard to get the word out because I was trying not to laugh. Dad looked genuinely disappointed and was worriedly swirling his spoon about in his yogurt.

'I hope you haven't put any spiders in

MY breakfast!' he said. 'You know I'm a vegetarian! This is really disgraceful behavior Mirabelle. I'm hoping for better from you this year at Witch School.'

By half past eight Wilbur and I were ready by the front door with our broomsticks.

'Have a lovely first day back at school!' said Mum as she kissed us both goodbye.

'And remember to behave yourselves,' said Dad.

'I always behave myself!' said Wilbur indignantly.

'I'm not talking to you,' said Dad and stared pointedly at me.

Chapter TWO

Wilbur and I flew up into the air and
flew side by side across the town that
we live in. It was a misty morning and it
felt wonderful to be out in the fresh air,
whizzing along, high in the sky. When we
came to the edge of the town we split up,
heading in different directions.

'Bye Wilbur!' I called as he

disappeared into the fog. 'Have a nice day at wizard school!'

'See you later,' said Wilbur, but he didn't sound quite as cheerful as usual. He was obviously still annoyed about the spider on his toast.

I pulled my school regulation hat down more firmly over my head because

it was windy, and held on tightly to Violet
as I flew on towards the deep dark forest
and Miss Spindlewick's Witch School
for Girls. I soon saw it looming up from
between the trees—a tall, grey building
with pointy roofs shaped like witch's
hats. Right now they were wreathed in
a ribbon of fog. I could see other young

21

witches flying towards the school on their broomsticks, coming from all different directions and I felt a shiver run up and down my spine. I LOVE my witch school. It makes me feel scared and excited all at the same time! I pointed my broomstick towards the playground below and landed with a bump and a skid on the black tarmac. Then I heard my name 'Mirabelle!' and turned to see my best friend Carlotta running towards me with her black kitten Midnight scampering along behind her.

'I missed you over the holidays!' she said, enveloping me in a great squeezy hug.

'I missed you too!' I said. 'It was so boring being apart! How was your holiday at the Witch Resort?'

'Oh well . . . it was pretty magical actually,' Carlotta admitted. 'I wish you could have come too though. It was so far away we had to go on an *aeroplane* to get there.

The hotel was in the mountains. There was a bubbling cauldron hot tub and an all you can eat witch food buffet!'

I wrinkled my nose at the idea of the buffet and clutched on tightly to my lunch box. Witch food is disgusting and I always bring my own lunch to school.

'I bought you something from my holiday!' said Carlotta and rummaged in her schoolbag. She brought out a small potion bottle full of glittering iridescent powder.

'I found it in the souvenir shop,' she said. 'I know you like collecting pretty potion bottles.'

'I do!' I said 'Thank you!' I turned
the bottle over in my hands, marveling
at the sparkling dust inside. It seemed to
shimmer in every colour of the rainbow.

'What does it do?' I asked.

'I'm not sure,' said Carlotta. 'The label is in a different language. But there's a picture of Rapunzel on the front, look! I thought maybe it was something to do with hair!'

'Maybe it will make my hair grow really long!' I said excitedly.

'Or make it change colour!' suggested Carlotta. 'But you should probably show it to your mum before you use it. I bet she'll know what it does. She's an expert in potion making isn't she?'

I nodded. Mum and Dad have their own beauty business, concocting face creams, perfumes, and lipsticks. Mum can spend hours up in her 'witch turret'

experimenting with ingredients. Dad
oversees to make sure everything is
natural and then adds his special fairy
touch at the end.

'You better hide it!' hissed Carlotta
suddenly and I looked up
to see our teacher, Miss
Spindlewick, coming
towards us. Hurriedly,
I slipped the potion
bottle into the pocket
of my skirt and tried to
look innocent. We are
not allowed to bring in
magic ingredients from
home. If we do, we are

supposed to hand it in at the beginning of the day.

'Good morning young witches!' said Miss Spindlewick and glanced down at Violet who was sitting on my shoulder.

She has never been too fond of Violet ever since she accidentally burned a hole in the register at the beginning of last term. It wasn't her fault. She was just excited.

'Good morning Miss Spindlewick,' I said and felt the palms of my hands get sweaty. Miss Spindlewick is very strict and she can be a bit frightening when she's cross. She's tall and thin with long, straight purple hair, a sharp chin and a *very* pointy nose. She likes to poke her spiky nose into *everything* that's going on.

'I do hope you're both going to behave yourselves this year,' said Miss Spindlewick fixing both Carlotta and me with a piercing stare. 'No more tricks in the classroom.'

'No tricks in the classroom!' said Carlotta.

'We promise!' I said. And in that moment, with the shadow of Miss Spindlewick looming over us, I really did mean it.

Chapter THREE

Our first lesson was potions. My
favourite! I watched in excitement as
Miss Spindlewick handed out a shiny new
cauldron to every pair of witches in the
room. These cauldrons were bigger than
the baby ones we had been allowed to
use last year. I poked my head right into
mine and Carlotta's, disappearing into the

velvety blackness.

'Can you heeear me?' I said. My voice sounded all strange and echoey as it bounced off the inside walls.

'Head out of your cauldron Mirabelle!' snapped Miss Spindlewick

as she walked past. I quickly took my head out of the cauldron and glanced at Carlotta who was trying not to laugh.

'Mirabelle!' whispered Carlotta. 'We really do have to try and be good this year. We promised!'

'I know,' I said. 'I'm sorry. I forgot! I'll try harder from now on.'

'Right!' said Miss Spindlewick from the front of the class. 'Today we are going to learn how to make a colour changing potion.'

'Ooh,' said the class.

'If you make it correctly,' said Miss Spindlewick, 'then you should be able to change the colour of this rose with just

a splash of the mixture.' She
held up a red rose in a vase
that had been sitting on the
corner of her desk.

'Once you've made your potion
you will come up and take it in turns
to put a drop of it on this rose. The more
drastically you can change the colour, the
higher your mark will be.'

She put the rose gently back down on
the desk.

'You may open your spell books at
page eighty seven and begin!'

There was a riffling of pages around
the classroom as everyone opened their
spell books.

'This doesn't look too hard,' said Carlotta.

'I'll go and get the ingredients from the cupboard,' I said, jumping off my stool and hurrying over to the big store cupboard where all the jars and bottles were kept. I had to wait a little bit as everyone else was also trying to get their ingredients too but at last I was able to squirm in and get all the things we needed. There were so many little bottles that I had to put some of them in my pockets in order to get them back to the desk. Meanwhile, Miss Spindlewick had turned off the lights and was busy lighting candles all around the room.

'For atmosphere,' she explained.

'Witch magic always works best with
a bit of atmosphere.'

'I think witch magic works best when you can see what you're doing,' whispered Carlotta as she now strained to read the shadowy page of the spell book.

We started to make our potion, throwing in a bit of this and a sprinkle of that, being careful to weigh the ingredients on an old fashioned set of scales.

'It's looking right so far,' said Carlotta as we both peered into the cauldron. 'Nice and bubbly!'

'We need a whole bottle of unicorn horn dust to finish it off,' I said reading the last ingredient in the spell book. I picked up a small, pretty bottle of shimmering rainbow-y dust and tossed the whole lot into the cauldron.

'Perfect!' said Carlotta and we both grinned at each other in the candlelight. Our potion began to fizz and froth in front of us, throwing up little sparks into the air.

'Is it supposed to fizz?' I asked after a moment. 'It doesn't say anything about fizzing in the spell book.'

'I'm sure it's fine,' said Carlotta. 'Let's take a little bit out and put it in a vial so we can test it on the rose! That's what it says to do here.'

I squinted down at the instructions.

'Take a glass vial and pour a little of the green mixture into it,' I read out loud. Then I frowned.

'Carlotta,' I said. 'Our mixture isn't green. It's purple!'

'What do you mean?' said Carlotta, peering into the cauldron. 'It probably just looks like that in the candlelight.'

'No,' I said. 'It's definitely purple!'

We both stepped back as our potion began to fizz and froth more violently, bubbling over and splattering onto the desk. Carlotta stared at me with wide eyes.

'Mirabelle,' she whispered. 'I think you made a mistake.'

'Me!?' I said indignantly. 'How could I have? We followed all the instructions!'

Carlotta pointed at the empty bottle of unicorn horn dust sitting on the desk.

'You poured the wrong bottle in,' she said. 'That's the bottle I brought you back from holiday!'

'It can't be!' I said, thrusting my hand into my pocket and bringing out a very similar bottle with a label on it saying 'unicorn horn.' I stared at it in horror and my heart started to beat very fast.

'They must have got mixed up in your pocket when you were carrying all the bottles back to the desk!' said Carlotta. 'Oh Mirabelle! What are we going to do?'

'I don't know!' I whispered, feeling panicked.

We took another step back from the cauldron as the potion began to fizz and froth even more, spitting globules of purple gloop across the room.

'Oh no! Oh no!' I cried. 'This is bad Carlotta!' The potion was going everywhere. It was spitting so far that it was landing on the heads of all the other witches in the room. Including Miss Spindlewick. A few drops splashed onto her head and she looked up from her desk. 'WHAT is going on?' she said, reaching up to wipe the potion off her hair. Then she spotted our cauldron, shaking and groaning and spluttering and her eyebrows shot up so high that they almost disappeared into her hair. She leapt up off her chair and pointed towards the door.

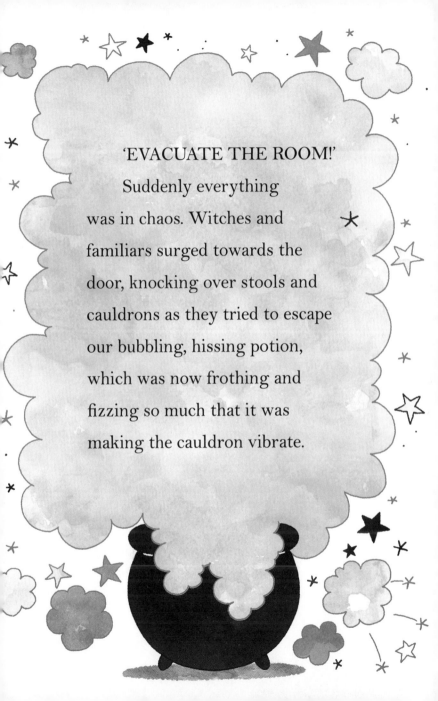

'EVACUATE THE ROOM!'

Suddenly everything
was in chaos. Witches and
familiars surged towards the
door, knocking over stools and
cauldrons as they tried to escape
our bubbling, hissing potion,
which was now frothing and
fizzing so much that it was
making the cauldron vibrate.

Before the first of my classmates reached the door there was an almighty BANG, a flash of purple light, and a sudden smell of violet scented shampoo. I closed my eyes tight as a shower of potion landed all over me and when I opened them I saw that

mine and Carlotta's cauldron had split right in two. We stared at each other in horrified silence. Everyone and everything in the classroom was covered in splatters of purple potion and all the candles had gone out. Miss Spindlewick turned on the light.

'It's too late!' she said. 'The damage is done. Everyone back to your desks!' All the witches in the room filed back to their chairs looking worried. Miss Spindlewick glared at me and Carlotta. She looked so angry that her face had gone almost as purple as her hair and her eyes looked like two tiny black raisins. I shrank back down into my chair.

'Mirabelle Starspell and Carlotta Cobweb,' said Miss Spindlewick. 'You are in BIG trouble!'

I stared up at Miss Spindlewick and gulped. She looked *furious*. Furious and . . . different. As I looked at her I noticed there was something strange about Miss Spindlewick. At first I couldn't work out what it was but then I realized. Her hair! It was much longer than before. It was almost down to the backs of her knees! And it seemed to be still growing . . .

Chapter FOUR

'My *hair!*' Miss Spindlewick screeched
from across the room. 'I've only just had
it cut!'

'What's happening to *my hair?*'
shrieked someone else.

Miss Spindlewick's hands flew to
her head. She looked down and gasped in
shock as she saw that her own hair had

now reached the floor and was staring to trail along behind her.

'WHAT did you put in that potion?' she demanded as the room erupted with squeals of horror. My head started to tingle and I looked down to see my own hair starting to grow too. It was growing fast! Snaking away across the floor. Hurriedly, I scrabbled to find the empty potion bottle and held it out towards Miss Spindlewick.

'It was my fault,' I gabbled. 'I put this in by mistake! I meant to put in the unicorn horn!'

Miss Spindlewick turned the little bottle over in her hands, frowning.

'I don't believe we have this particular *joke shop* potion in the store cupboard,' she said. 'Where, may I ask, did you get it from?'

I hung my head, not wanting to get Carlotta into any more trouble but before I could make something up she squeaked, 'I gave it to Mirabelle! I bought it on my holiday!'

'I see,' said Miss Spindlewick

sounding as though she didn't see at all.

'I swear I didn't do it on purpose!' I said. 'It was a mistake! I got mixed up because I couldn't see what I was doing properly in the candlelight!'

Miss Spindlewick raised an eyebrow.

'Magic from home is not permitted at school,' she said. 'You should have handed this in to me at the beginning of the day and collected it at home time.'

'I know,' I said. 'I'm really sorry. I thought it would be OK in my pocket.'

'Miss Spindlewick!' came a panicked voice from the other side of the room. 'My hair! It won't stop growing.'

'Nor will anyone's, Lavinia!' snapped Miss Spindlewick as she turned and shuffled back to her desk, through the mass of hair that was now covering the whole floor. Miss Spindlewick had miles and miles of hair coming from her head.

It was getting tangled in the desks and chairs as she walked. And everyone else in the classroom was getting tangled up too. There was hair everywhere!

'Please Miss Spindlewick,' came another voice. 'Can you make a reversing potion?'

'I'm afraid not Hazel,' said Miss Spindlewick as she sat down on the corner of her desk and crossed her arms. 'I don't have the right kind of ingredients to make a reversing spell for this sort of *joke* potion. We must merely sit and wait for our hair to stop growing and then . . .' she reached down into the drawer at the side if her desk and brought out a pair of huge, shiny scissors 'We'll all have to have haircuts.'

'Oh my stars!' I whispered to Carlotta. 'Everyone's going to hate us. Miss Spindlewick doesn't know anything about cutting hair!'

'Everyone *is* going to hate us,' agreed Carlotta despondently.

'But what if it never stops growing?' shouted Hazel.

'What if it *drowns* us!' yelped Lavinia. 'I don't want to drown in a roomful of hair!'

'It won't drown us,' said Miss Spindlewick. 'It's slowing down already. Just give it a few more minutes.'

We all sat and waited in silence.
I heard the bell go for lunchtime in the
distance but still nobody moved. Nobody
could move! The weight of hair coming
from our heads was too heavy.

'Right!' said Miss Spindlewick, at
last. 'Me first!' she took the
scissors and measured
her hair down to
her waist. Then
SNIP, SNIP. The
blades of the
scissors flashed
in the light from
the window.

'Much better!' said Miss Spindlewick. 'If a bit jagged . . . right, who is next!' She gave a witchy cackle and then stopped herself when she saw the sea of dismayed faces.

'Hazel first!' she said and advanced towards Hazel's desk. Carlotta and I watched as Miss Spindlewick went round the whole room. SNIP, SNIP, SNIP.

'You've cut mine too short Miss Spindlewick!' complained Lavinia.

'Mine's wonky!' cried someone else.

At last only Carlotta and I were left.

'Right,' said Miss Spindlewick, glancing up at the clock on the wall. 'Everyone else go for lunch! I'm going to

deal with these two.'

I felt Carlotta begin to shake next to me as the rest of the class shuffled through the piles of cut hair towards the door, glaring at us on their way out.

'Oh, Miss Spindlewick!' cried Carlotta, bursting into tears. 'We really didn't mean to cause all this trouble!'

'I promise we didn't,' I said, starting to feel a bit scared too.

'Hmm,' said Miss Spindlewick. 'I've a mind to cut ALL your hair off as a punishment!'

'No!' screamed Carlotta. 'Please, Miss Spindlewick!'

'Unfortunately, I don't think your parents would be very happy, so I won't,' said Miss Spindlewick. 'But I AM going to insist that you both stay back and sweep up all this hair. Without magic.'

'Without magic?' I gasped.

Miss Spindlewick gave me a hard stare.

'Of course Miss Spindlewick,' I mumbled.

'You will stay in here as long as it takes to tidy up,' said Miss Spindlewick. 'Even if it means missing lunch.'

'Yes Miss Spindlewick,' we both said.

'Good,' Miss Spindlewick replied. 'Now sit still both of you, I'm going to cut

61

your hair before I go for my lunch.
How long was yours before Mirabelle?'

★ ★ ★

Ten minutes later, Carlotta and I were
alone in the classroom on our hands and
knees, gathering up all the hair into piles
and putting it into big bin bags while the
wind howled outside the windows of the
classroom.

'This is awful,' said Carlotta. 'And I'm hungry. I'm not allowed to go to the cafeteria until all this is done. This is all your fault Mirabelle!'

'*My* fault?' I said. 'You were the one who gave me the potion bottle!'

'YOU were the one who put it into the cauldron!' said Carlotta. 'And I thought you would be pleased that I bought you a present back from holiday!'

'I am,' I said. 'I'm being unfair, I'm sorry. You're right, it *is* my fault.'

'You promised we wouldn't get into trouble this term and now look at us!' said Carlotta.

'I know,' I said, hanging my head. 'I'm sorry. It was a mistake though. I really didn't mean to get the potions mixed up.'

Carlotta didn't say anything and I knew that she was still upset. I hate it when we argue.

'You can share my lunch,' I said and fetched it from my bag. I handed one sandwich to Carlotta and took a bite of the other one. Mmm, fairy honey! Dad always makes mine and Wilbur's packed lunches, they're the best.

'It's quite sweet isn't it,' said Carlotta,

wrinkling her nose. Carlotta is full witch and doesn't appreciate the tastiness of fairy food. I took another bite.

CRUNCH.

What was that? There was something in my mouth and it didn't taste or feel like honey. It felt crispy and hairy and . . .

'ARGGGGHHH!' I shouted and spat my mouthful onto the floor. I could see long spindly legs! A hairy body!

'ARGH!' I shouted again and took a mouthful of water from my flask, swishing it around my mouth. Suddenly I felt very sick.

'What's the matter?' said Carlotta. 'It's only a spider. They're delicious!'

'They're . . . DISGUSTING!' I said, feeling my face go hot. I couldn't believe I had just had one of mum's crisped spiders in my mouth! It had felt HORRIBLE.

'I bet Wilbur sneaked it into my sandwich before we left for school!' I said. 'To get back at me!'

All of a sudden I realized how sick Wilbur must have felt at breakfast that morning when he discovered the spider on his toast and I felt a bit guilty. I decided I would try and make it up to him when

I got home.

'I wish there was a spider in *my* sandwich!' said Carlotta wistfully as she pulled apart the pieces of bread to have a look. 'Nope, no spider! Just sweet, sticky fairy honey . . .'

We only had a couple of minutes of lunchtime left by the time we had finished tidying up, but at least Carlotta had cheered up again.

'I know you didn't really mean to use the wrong potion Mirabelle,' she said as we made our way out to the playground. 'I'm sorry I said it was all your fault.'

'That's OK,' I said as I linked arms with her. 'But I'm going to be super extra careful to not cause any more trouble today.'

'Yes . . . at least wait until you get home!' Carlotta grinned.

Chapter FIVE

Miss Spindlewick was waiting for us in the playground with the rest of the class. It was the last lesson of the day. Flying!

'It has got extremely windy today witches,' said Miss Spindlewick as she licked her finger and held it up in the air. 'So we are going to go into the forest and practice our loop the loops closer to

the ground or else we'll all end
up blown into the misty murky
millpond. No one is allowed to
fly higher than the tops of the
trees! Do you understand?'

'Yes, Miss Spindlewick,'
chanted the class. We all followed
her out of the playground and
into the deep dark forest that
surrounded the school. I got onto
my broomstick and rose up into
the air. I'm really good at flying
actually because I practice a lot
at home. I don't need lessons.

Swoosh! I did a perfect loop the loop in the air.

Swoosh, swoosh! I can even do it with my eyes closed . . .

CRASH!

'Hey Mirabelle!' shouted Lavinia as we both tumbled to the ground. 'Watch where you're going!'

'Sorry!' I said, moving away from her. But now I was too close to someone else. There wasn't enough room for us all do be doing loop the loops so close to the ground. I rose a little higher on my broomstick. I wouldn't go past the tops of the trees, just level with them. That wouldn't be breaking the rules would it?

As I rose higher into the air I felt the wind begin to pull me. But I'm strong and a really good flyer.

'Wheee!' I did a perfect loop the loop as the wind whipped though my hair. And then another one and another one. Loop the loops are my favourite!

'Mirabelle!' came a voice from below and I saw Carlotta staring up at me.

'You're too high!' she said. 'Come down lower!'

'It's fine!' I said, 'Miss Spindlewick hasn't even noticed! She's behind a tree over there helping Hazel!'

'That's not the point!' hissed Carlotta from down below. 'You promised you wouldn't break the rules again!'

'I'm not . . .' I began.

But then suddenly there was a huge gust of

wind that blew me sideways and I found
myself hurtling across the tops of the
trees in the direction of the misty murky
millpond.

'Uh oh,' I said as I gripped onto my broomstick and tried to lower it back into the trees. But Miss Spindlewick had been right. The wind really was very strong and I found myself buffeted this way and that until a powerful gust suddenly knocked me off my broomstick altogether. I managed to grab onto the handle with one hand and there I hung for a few moments, swinging backwards and forwards in the wind.

'Uh oh,' I said again as my hat blew right off my head. I watched in dismay as it swirled and twirled over the tops of the trees until it landed with a small 'plop' in the misty, murky millpond. I needed to get it back! Miss Spindlewick would be furious! But she would be even more furious if she knew I was flying above the tops of the trees. With a great amount of effort I managed to scrabble back onto my broomstick and then point it down, landing with a skid on the forest floor, away from my classmates. I could hear them all still doing loop the loops though the trees and I hoped that Miss Spindlewick hadn't noticed that I had disappeared.

I started to run as
fast as I could, towards the
millpond. I would just quickly
collect my hat and then hurry
back to the class. Violet flapped
along beside me, blowing anxious puffs of
smoke out from her snout.

'Maybe you can just fly into the
middle of the pond to collect the hat?'
I suggested. 'There are no rules about
dragons going near the millpond!'

Violet snorted out an indignant flame
of purple fire.

Just as we were about to reach the
millpond I heard a high-pitched squeal
coming from above that made me jump.

'What was that?' I said, grabbing Violet out of the air and clutching her to my chest. I looked up and saw a row of black crows staring down at me from a branch above but the squeal hadn't sounded like a crow. Then I noticed a movement through the branches in the sky above and my heart leapt into my mouth. It was Carlotta! She was blowing about in the wind above the trees, heading in the same direction as my hat. Towards the millpond!

'Oh no!' I cried. 'Carlotta wait there!' and without thinking I leapt back onto my broomstick, rising up into the sky as fast as I could.

But it was impossible for Carlotta to stay still. The wind was too strong. It had blown her off her broomstick and she was hanging onto it with both hands, soaring through the air, flapping and swirling towards the misty murky millpond. Now that I was above the tops of the trees again, I was getting blown about too.

'Carlotta!' I cried, as I struggled to stay on my broom. 'Grab onto my hand!'

'I can't!' shouted Carlotta as she was buffeted away from me and downwards

towards the millpond. 'I can't reach you!'

I was starting to lose control too

now.

83

'Violet, fly back and get Miss Spindlewick,' I cried. I hunched down low on my broomstick and wrapped my arms around it so that I wouldn't fall off. I closed my eyes tightly as I spun and twirled in the same direction as Carlotta. And then *'splash!'* I heard her fall into the water!

'Don't worry Carlotta, I'm coming!' I yelled

'Splash!' In I went after her.

I gasped as my head disappeared into the dark, murky water. It was icy cold and I could feel slimy pondweed waving about near my feet. I grit my teeth together and kicked my legs hard, swimming across to where my best friend was splashing and flailing nearby. I hugged her around the chest and then with all my strength I dragged her to the bank where we both grabbed onto a tree root, panting for breath.

'What were you doing?' I asked.
'You shouldn't have been flying above the treetops!'

'I was following you,' said Carlotta.
'I was worried you were going to get blown away! What were you doing following me into the millpond?'

'I couldn't just let you drown!' I said.
'I know you can't swim.' For a moment I felt very lucky to be half fairy. Fairies love nature and swimming in wild streams is one of their favourite things to do. Dad taught me to swim when I was very young.

We both looked at each other and smiled, before pulling ourselves back up to

the bank just as Violet came into
sight through the trees, riding with
Miss Spindlewick on her broom.

'Mirabelle Starspell and Carlotta
Cobweb!' said Miss Spindlewick angrily.
'What in the name of *bats and spiders* has
been going on now?'

'It was all my fault,' I said. 'It really was! Don't get cross with Carlotta, she was trying to save me.'

'Mirabelle saved ME!' said Carlotta. 'I'm just glad Midnight wasn't on the broomstick too.'

'But I flew up above the trees first,' I said. 'Miss Spindlewick, it really was my fault. I went maybe a little bit too high and got blown away. Carlotta was just trying to rescue me. And then she got blown away and . . .'

Miss Spindlewick glittered down at us with black eyes.

'I don't care who did what,' she said. 'You're both in trouble! Mirabelle, you

should have stayed near to the forest floor!
Carlotta, you should have come to me
instead of going after Mirabelle yourself!'

'There wasn't time,' said Carlotta in
a small voice.

'Hmm,' said Miss Spindlewick. 'Well I do have to commend you on trying to rescue one another—that was brave. And you were right to send Violet to get me Mirabelle, but the fact of the matter is that neither of you have been paying attention to the rules today. Especially you Mirabelle!'

'I know,' I said guiltily. 'It's just that there are so many!'

'The rules are there for a reason,' said Miss Spindlewick. 'If you had given

that potion bottle to me at the beginning
of the day, you wouldn't have made a
mistake and caused so much trouble in
the potions class this morning. If you had
obeyed the rules about not flying higher
than the trees then neither of you would
have ended up in the pond.'

'I know,' I said. 'I'm
sorry.'

Then I burst into
tears because I couldn't
help it.

'I know I
sometimes DO cause
mischief on purpose,'
I sobbed. 'But today I

really didn't mean to do anything naughty! And everything still went wrong. I even had a spider in my sandwich at lunchtime!'

Miss Spindlewick put her hand on my shoulder.

'No lasting harm was done today thank goodness. But remember, the rules are there for your own good. You need to make sure you follow them!'

'I'll try harder,' I promised.

'Good,' said Miss Spindlewick. 'I'll take your broomsticks, and you two can go back inside and get dry.'

Carlotta and I both looked at each other in surprise. Were we going to get away with this without a punishment?

We started to back away slowly from Miss
Spindlewick, turning in the direction of the
school.

'And you can both have lunchtime
detentions for the rest of the week,' came
Miss Spindlewick's voice from behind
us. 'You can clean out all the cauldrons
after potion class.
Without magic!'

'I knew
it,' whispered
Carlotta.

Chapter SIX

Together we walked through the trees, back towards the school.

'I am sorry I got you into trouble today,' I said. 'None of this would have happened if I HAD properly followed the rules.'

'It's all right,' said Carlotta. 'I'd rather be having detention with you than have to hang out with Lavinia and Hazel anyway! I'm just going to make sure my mum makes me a really nice packed lunch for our lunchtime detentions. Lots of spider sandwiches!'

'Yuck!' I said.

Luckily, by home time the wind had died down a bit so I was able to leave school on my broomstick. (Sometimes, if the weather is bad I have to wait for Mum and Dad to come and collect me in the car.) I waved goodbye to Carlotta and then kicked off into the air, rising up above the trees and flying towards the edge of the forest and out to the town. As I flew, I noticed

a speck in the distance coming from a
different direction. It was Wilbur!

'Hi!' I said when he got close.

'Hi,' said Wilbur.

We flew along in silence for a bit.

Wilbur didn't seem in a very chatty mood.

'I'm going to make you a treat when we get home!' I said after a few minutes of silence. 'A big ice cream with all the fairy food I can find!'

'No thanks,' said Wilbur. 'I don't trust you to make me anything to eat!'

'I swear I won't put a spider in it!' I said, as we got near to our house and floated down to the front door step.

'No, that's OK,' Wilbur said. 'I'll make my own.'

'But I WANT to make it for you!' I said, starting to feel a bit cross. 'I want to make up for putting the spider on your toast. You should be grateful that I'M not

more upset about you putting
a spider in MY lunchbox!'

Mum opened the door.

'Hello my darlings!'
she said.

'I didn't put a spider in your lunchbox!' said Wilbur. 'I wouldn't do that!'

'You wouldn't?' I said.

'Of course not!' said Wilbur.

He pushed past me into the house and I noticed that Mum was looking a bit shifty.

'MUM!' I shouted.

Mum bit her lip.

'I'm sorry Mirabelle,' she said.

'I couldn't resist after your trick on

Wilbur this morning. You know I like my practical jokes. And spider sandwiches really *are* delicious!'

'But it wasn't funny,' I said, feeling hurt. 'Honestly Mum, I've had SUCH a bad day! First I accidentally made everyone's hair grow and then I accidentally ended up in the misty murky millpond with Carlotta!'

'Oh, Mirabelle, it sounds as though you have a lot to tell me,' Mum said with her eyebrows raised. 'I'm sorry you're upset. You're right, it was quite wrong of me to put that spider in your sandwich and I promise I won't do it again. Let's hope you don't do it again either.

Now, why don't I make it up to you.
I can make you and Wilbur big ice cream
sundaes, and you can tell me all about your
day. How does that sound?'

'Good,' I sniffed. 'But I don't know
if I trust you.'

'Of course you can trust me,' said
Mum, pulling me in for a big hug.

'OK, but *I* want to make the sundae
for Wilbur,' I said, following Mum into the
kitchen.

We got big glass bowls and filled
them with ice cream, butterscotch,
sprinkles, and sugared rose petals while
I told Mum about my day.

'How long did you say Miss

Spindlewick's hair was?!' said Mum,
astounded. 'And I suppose a week's worth
of detention for the flying debacle *is* fair!

And isn't little Violet a special and brave dragon!'

Then I carried the ice creams regally out to the sitting room where Wilbur was busy watching his favourite Wizard's game show programme.

'Look Wilbur,' I said proudly. 'I made you this!'

Wilbur looked suspiciously at the ice cream that I was holding out to him but I saw his eyes grow big and wide. I knew he

wouldn't be able to
resist a special fairy
sundae.

'No spiders?'
he asked.

'No spiders!' I
said. 'I PROMISE!'

Wilbur took the
ice cream and I sat down
next to him on the sofa. Together we
started to eat them.

'Yum,' said Wilbur. 'This is delicious!
Thanks Mirabelle.'

'That's OK Wilbur. And I promise,
no more spiders on toast.' I smiled happily.
It felt nice to do nice things for people.

From now on, I decided,
I was going to try and be good and
always follow the rules.

Well, *almost* always.

Turn the page
for some
mischievous
things to make
and do!

Squished Spider Biscuits!

Mirabelle's mum is a witch and loves to eat witchy food like toast with spiders sprinkled on top. Why not impress your witchy friends with these delicious Squished Spider Biscuits?

(Remember to always ask a grown-up to help when you're baking.)

Ingredients

- ★ 300 grams of plain flour
- ★ 150 grams of unsalted butter
- ★ ¼ teaspoon salt
- ★ 150 grams of caster sugar
- ★ 1 teaspoon of vanilla extract
- ★ 1 egg
- ★ Two big handfuls of raisins (these will be your squished spiders)
- ★ 2 teaspoons of icing sugar

Equipment

- ⭐ Mixing bowl
- ⭐ Wooden spoon
- ⭐ Baking tray
- ⭐ Baking parchment
- ⭐ Rolling pin
- ⭐ Cookie cutter
- ⭐ Cling film

Method:

1. Wash your hands.

2. Mix the flour, salt and sugar in a large mixing bowl.

3. Add the butter and rub it in with your fingers until the mixture looks like fine breadcrumbs.

4. Beat the egg and stir it into the dry ingredients with the vanilla extract.

5. Knead the mixture to make a smooth dough – add a splash of milk if it's looking too dry.

6. Add the raisins and knead all together.

7. Wrap the dough in cling film and pop it in the fridge to chill for 15-20 minutes.

8. Preheat the oven to 180C/160C fan and line a baking tray with the baking parchment.

9. Roll out the dough on a floured surface to about 5mm thick and cut out your biscuit shapes with the cookie cutter.

10. Put your biscuits on the baking tray and then put them in the oven for 15 minutes.

11. When they are lightly golden, they are ready. Take the biscuits out of the oven and leave to cool.

12. Once cooled, you can sprinkle a little bit of icing sugar over the top.

Magic Pets!

Witches often have a familiar – a special sidekick,
by their side at all times. Mirabelle has a little dragon
called Violet and Carlotta has a kitten called Midnight.

Answer these questions to find out
what your familiar would be.

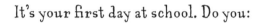

It's your first day at school. Do you:

A. Slip into the classroom unnoticed and quietly appraise
your classmates?

B. Bound in, excited to get started?

C. Swoop in, telling your new friends all about yourself?

D. Slink in, sit at your desk, and have a nice big stretch?

It's time for PE and you are
taking part in a race. Do you:

A. Take your time but always get there in the end, with style?

B. Bound off at top speed but get distracted by
a leaf blowing in the wind, and go off course?

C. Race off with a burst of speed and don't
let anyone get in your way?

D. Preen yourself at the start line before setting off.
You are graceful and quick?

It's parents' evening!
What will the teacher say about you?

A. You are intelligent, calm and very observant.

B. You are the funny one in the class,
but you are easily distracted.

C. You have strong opinions and you aren't afraid
to express them in class.

D. You are kind and confident, with a relaxed attitude
when it comes to schoolwork.

Results

Mostly As

Your familiar is a gecko! With huge inquisitive eyes, and a
talent for blending in with its surroundings, your familiar
often notices things other people don't.

Mostly Bs

Your familiar is a puppy! Playful and full of energy, your
puppy familiar is a loyal friend who will never leave your side.

Mostly Cs

Your familiar is a dragon! Your dragon matches your fiery
personality and together you are unstoppable.

Mostly Ds

Your familiar is a kitten! Sleek and graceful, your kitten
likes to perch on your shoulder and keep you
toasty warm when it's cold outside.

Wordsearch!

Mirabelle has hidden the following words in this wordsearch. Can you use your finding skills to spot them all?

Mirabelle

Carlotta

Violet

witch

fairy

magic

midnight

A	G	I	W	I	T	C	H	Z	Q	L
C	P	O	Y	E	R	K	J	E	O	I
W	K	D	G	A	S	Y	U	E	P	Z
A	Q	C	A	R	L	O	T	T	A	R
J	D	A	B	N	X	K	E	U	C	M
G	L	J	A	S	R	I	V	G	K	F
M	I	D	N	I	G	H	T	P	O	A
I	S	Y	D	O	Z	Q	M	F	S	I
R	E	V	A	H	T	J	S	P	Y	R
A	C	R	U	I	X	N	V	O	A	Y
B	U	F	L	P	M	D	E	S	J	F
E	F	T	V	H	I	A	U	E	C	S
L	K	A	O	G	M	S	G	S	O	H
L	Q	W	N	U	F	E	S	I	P	Y
E	A	S	V	I	O	L	E	T	C	L
M	G	B	M	K	E	A	H	J	X	S

Have you read . . .

From the world of ISADORA MOON

MIRABELLE

Gets up to Mischief

Half witch, half fairy, totally naughty!

Harriet Muncaster

Chapter ONE

'NO witchy magic!' said Dad, wagging his finger at me. It was Saturday morning and we were all in the dining room together having breakfast. Me, my mum, my dad, and my brother Wilbur.

'Remember,' said Dad, 'this is a fairy celebration, the most important one in the whole year! I don't want to see any of your

witchy things at the midsummer dance tonight. No cauldrons, no potion bottles. No pointy witch or wizard hats!'

'No cauldrons!' I gasped. 'But I always take my travelling potion kit with me, wherever I go!'

'I know,' said Dad. 'And it always seems to cause a lot of mischief.'

'Mischief?' I said trying to look surprised.

'Yes,' said Dad. 'And I don't want any naughtiness at the midsummer's ball this year. You must embrace your fairy side for the night. Why don't you dust off your fairy wand? I never see you using it.'

'That's because it's rubbish!' I complained. 'It only does . . . boring magic.'

Dad raised his eyebrows at me and his fairy wings fluttered in annoyance. I had almost said 'good magic' but stopped myself just in time.

'Dad's right,' chipped in Mum. 'You and Wilbur must embrace your fairy side for the night.' she smiled at us with her dark purple lips. 'You are both half fairy after all.'

Wilbur sighed. He hates being reminded that he's half fairy. He finds it embarrassing and would prefer to be full wizard. I don't mind so much. It can be useful for getting out of trouble. People never expect fairies to be naughty!

'We will *all* do our best to be as "fairy" as possible for Dad,' said

Mum and I stared at her in surprise. Mum is a full blown witch and I could never imagine her trying to be 'fairy,' she loves whisking around on her broomstick and cackling and making potions. Sometimes she can even be quite mischievous too!

'That's settled then!' said Dad. He took a sip of his flower-nectar tea and looked at us all happily over the rim of the mug. Mum crunched down on her spider-sprinkled toast.

I looked back at them and thought about how happy it would make Dad if Wilbur, Mum and I embraced our fairy sides for the night. I decided that I would try my absolute best to be good. No potions, no cauldrons and no pointed hats!

Harriet Muncaster

Harriet Muncaster, that's me! I'm the
author and illustrator of two young fiction
series, Mirabelle and Isadora Moon.
I love anything teeny tiny, anything
starry, and everything glittery.

Love Mirabelle?
Why not try these too . . .

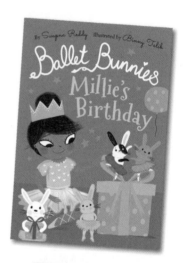